DON'T TURN OUT THE LIGHTS

A tribute to Alvin Schwartz's

SCARY STORIES TO TELL IN THE DARK

DON'T
OUT THE

A tribute to Alvin Schwartz's

SCARY STORIES TO TELL IN THE DARK

TURN

LIGHTS

Edited by

JONATHAN MABERRY

See p. 395 for a complete list of copyright information.

Library of Congress Control Number: 2020936261
ISBN 978-0-06-287767-3

Typography by Laura Mock
20 21 22 23 24   PC/LSCH   10 9 8 7 6 5 4 3 2 1

First Edition

This book is dedicated to Alvin Schwartz,
for scaring the snot out of generations
of young readers. And for making being
scared a whole bunch of fun!

And, as always, for Sara Jo.

CONTENTS

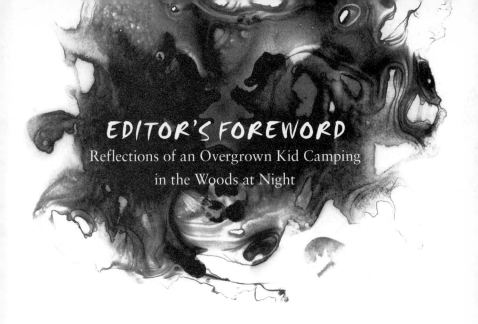

EDITOR'S FOREWORD
Reflections of an Overgrown Kid Camping in the Woods at Night

When I was a kid there were scary stories, but not *Scary Stories to Tell in the Dark*.

Those books were published in the '80s, when I was already in my early twenties. By then I was big and tough and worked as a bodyguard. I wasn't afraid of much. Not anymore.

But I remember being afraid.

I remember *liking* how that felt.

The ripples of goose bumps along my arms when there was a sound in the dark I couldn't identify. The sudden intake of breath when something fell over in my closet for no good reason. The jolt to my heart as a floorboard creaked when I knew for sure no one else was home.

I lived in an old row home, so . . . sure . . . the place groaned and moaned, and the rational part of my mind knew that there were logical explanations. Foundation settling. The wood frame sagging under the weight of years. A mouse behind the wall.

There are always explanations.

But that didn't stop me from being afraid.

Yeah, I really *liked* being afraid.

I watched scary movies even when I wasn't allowed. I read horror comics. And I spent a lot of time listening to my grandmother—we called her Nanny—tell spooky stories. She knew a lot of them. She was pretty spooky herself. Born on Halloween and, I think, about a million years old. Or at least, she seemed that old. Her face was all wrinkles and creases, but her eyes were young. Like a faerie or an imp pretending to be an elderly lady.

Her house was filled with books about vampires, werewolves, ghosts, and all kinds of things that went bump in the dark. If Luna Lovegood from the Harry Potter novels was someone's grandmother, that would be Nanny. I loved her. She was my favorite person.

She told me strange tales about haunted houses and monsters in closets and headless horsemen and crawly things that didn't have a name. She told me about lost souls and hungry ghouls and disembodied hands scuttling like spiders.

I used to think that she made those stories up, but

later on discovered that she only made *some* of them up. A lot of those tales were old. Older than her, in some cases. Tales that were handed down over the years, like creepy heirlooms. Campfire stories, urban legends, myths, and even versions of classic fiction. I first met Dracula in one of her stories, but the way she told it was different from the novel I later read. The same with *The Strange Case of Dr. Jekyll and Mr. Hyde*, *Frankenstein*, and *The Phantom of the Opera*. She reshaped these tales to fit her mood and her likes and her quirky sense of humor. And that was absolutely perfect.

I've since retold some of her tales to my sister's kids. Yes, I was the weird uncle who told spooky stories to my nephews. Proud of that, too.

I first encountered Alvin Schwartz's *Scary Stories to Tell in the Dark* in 1983. I was about to go camping alone and wanted something creepy to read. The salesman at the bookstore said that the book was filled with "campfire stories and weird stuff like that." He warned me that it was mostly for elementary readers, but I didn't care. I bought it, and the latest books by Stephen King and Robert McCammon.

I spent a week camping and canoeing in the Pine Barrens of New Jersey. It is a vast forest, and you can be completely alone and cut off from everyone in a five-minute walk from the banks of the stream. I paddled along the cedar-water streams and hiked the woods, and then spent some very pleasant hours scaring the absolute bejeezus out of myself reading those stories. King scared me, because Stephen King scares everyone. McCammon scared me because he knows exactly how to do that. But when I opened Schwartz's book, I expected to be amused but not actually scared. After all, I was a big, tough adult with black belts.

And yet . . .

There is something especially fascinating about spooky stories intended for young readers. There is a simplicity to them that is deceptive. Like an apple offered by a kindly old lady. Ask Snow White how that turned out.

Sure, the setting had a lot to do with it. All by myself in a night-dark forest, with ten thousand insects and animals out there watching me. This was years before cell phones were a thing. When you get lost in a forest like that, you are truly lost. You gain a whole new understanding of the word "alone."

Alvin Schwartz's stories genuinely creeped me out.

Some of them I even recognized as urban legends or folklore, but he gave them unnerving little twists. They were campfire tales, and I was huddled—with no one else around—by a campfire.

Sounds absurd, sure. Tough guy like me being spooked by stories for kids. But don't forget, the kid we used to be is still alive in all of us. And the civilized part of us is only one power failure, one bad storm, one unexplainable moment of strangeness away from being a primitive and terrified caveman.

When I got back from my trip—and, no, I was not attacked by pop-eyed goblins, giant spiders, or the ghost of a serial killer—I went looking for more of those books. Unfortunately I had to wait until Halloween of the following year to get *More Scary Stories to Tell in the Dark*. And then there was a gap of years before *Scary Stories 3: More Tales to Chill Your Bones* was published.

And after that . . . nothing. No more. Alvin Schwartz died the year after that third book was published. He was in his midsixties, not much older than I am now.

I left bodyguard work behind and became a college instructor (teaching martial arts history, women's self-defense, and jujutsu), then I ran a dojo, and soon I became a graphic artist. All of that was on the way to deciding to try my hand at writing my own scary stories. My first horror novel, *Ghost Road Blues*, was published in 2006, and I've written dozens of novels, short stories, and creepy comic books since then.

Over the years I've lost count of how many copies of the complete set of *Scary Stories* I've bought for friends. Not just for the *kids* of friends, but for any of my friends who like a creepy story well told. All of those copies could probably fill a truck. No, better yet, they could build a pretty cool fort to hide in on dark and stormy nights.

When the Horror Writers Association and Harper-Collins teamed up to do a tribute anthology, I was very excited. When they asked me to edit it, I was floored. I even got a little misty. Kind of wish Nanny was still with us . . . she'd be delighted.

I began reaching out to writers to see who might be interested. I was hoping that a few of the better authors I knew had heard of Alvin Schwartz's books. Or maybe had bought them for their own children. What I did not expect was that *all* of them knew and loved these stories. Everyone had a favorite, and some could recite them from memory. When I talk to booksellers and librarians about this new book, I see their eyes light up. Even today, all these years later, the Scary Stories books fly off the shelves. Every time I visit a library I check to see if there are copies . . . and I find new and old editions that have been read so many times they are falling to pieces.

This volume contains thirty-five original stories.

Most of them are short—like Schwartz's tales—and a few are longer, introducing younger readers to the standard short story form (but in a pretty creepy way!). All of them are delightful and spooky and downright weird.

I know that the new generation of readers will enjoy them and, hopefully, be skeeved out. And I am so happy to be able to share these new stories with the millions who either grew up with the original *Scary Stories* or folks like me who discovered them later and read them to the children in their lives.

So, if you're not camping in the deep dark woods, then wait until night has fallen, pull a sheet over your head, and read by flashlight. Let's all be kids again with these scary stories inspired by *the* Scary Stories that started it all.

—Jonathan Maberry, editor

THE FUNERAL PORTRAIT

By Laurent Linn

Terror was about to infect the kingdom, and panic spread like a virus.

Queen Benévola balanced on the edge of death and her only child, Malvino Mandamás, was next in line; he would become king. As intensely as the kind queen was beloved, her demoniac son, Mandamás, was despised. But the royal family wielded the power. Nothing could be done.

Or so everyone believed.

Señora Alma's acclaimed lineage reached as far back as the royal family's—she and her ancestors performed *one* solemn duty: painting the royal funeral portraits. And so, on her deathbed, knowing her long life was at its end, Queen Benévola summoned the revered portrait artist to fulfill her task.

Supported by a simple wooden cane and wrapped in a black shawl, the reclusive painter dutifully arrived at the palace to create the painting. Tales of old, wrinkled Señora Alma and her accomplished legacy spanned generations; some said she was one hundred years old, maybe even two. No matter her true age, she was distinctly skilled and painted the queen's Funeral Portrait with unparalleled speed, for just as Señora Alma applied her last dab of pigment to the canvas, the queen exhaled her last breath.

"How fortunate," Señora Alma said, "I was able to paint her while she was still alive."

Queen Benévola's remains rested in the Galería, a long hall with carved paneling and trembling candlelight. Most striking were the life-size oil paintings: centuries of royal Funeral Portraits that lined the walls of the gallery like a timeline of compassion, occasionally punctured by tyranny, all with penetrating painted eyes.

At the end was the Funeral Portrait of the queen's father, King Tirano, a despot who had ruled with vicious cruelty. His seething glare was chilling, even if only caught on canvas. But next to that, above her casket, now hung Queen Benévola's glorious Funeral Portrait: an uncanny likeness. While the folds of her turquoise gown had the illusion of being true velvet and the rubies of her crown looked like they reflected actual flame, the rendering of the queen herself stole one's breath. It was as if pulsing blood flowed through the applied pigments of her skin and a vivid spirit shone through her painted gaze.

When Señora Alma arrived in the Galería to pay her last respects, the gathered nobility and commoners showered the legendary painter with praise.

"You are too kind." Señora Alma admired her masterpiece. "I simply attempt to replicate in paint what I glean from the person's soul."

A noblewoman scowled up at the portrait of King Tirano. "You certainly gleaned what was in *him*!" She shuddered. "It's as if the painting stares through me."

Señora Alma frowned at the portrayal of the previous king that she had painted so many years before. "I captured him all too well, didn't I?"

A commanding voice boomed through the Galería. "Where's that woman?" Everyone turned—it was the newly crowned King Malvino Mandamás himself! Strutting beside him was his eleven-year-old son, Prince Consentido, who had the eyes of his grandmother but the bearing of his father.

"Señora Alma!" the new King Mandamás barked. "The way you've painted my mother is impressive." He put his hands on his hips. "You will paint *my* portrait."

The crowd gasped. Everyone knew the old proverb: it was perilous to have one's Funeral Portrait painted when one was in their prime.

Prince Consentido interrupted. "What about me? I want a portrait too!"

"Quiet!" Mandamás shoved his son away. "*I'm* the king."

"But, King Mandamás," a groveling court minister said. "What about the fate of your grandfather King Tirano! He had Señora Alma paint his portrait when *he* was young and look what happened. It brought the *curse!*"

A slight grin started to light on Señora Alma's face, but she quickly extinguished it and resumed her somber expression.

"You think *I* believe that stupidity?" King Mandamás said. "When my likeness hangs in this hall someday it shall resemble me *now*, when I'm young and handsome, not when I'm old and sickly." He waved his hand up at Queen Benévola's portrait.

Señora Alma bowed as low as her elderly bones would allow. "Sire, I cannot break from my family's tradition and will paint your Funeral Portrait only *once*. To capture you in your full glory, I must first observe what kind of ruler you will be."

King Mandamás huffed, then glanced up at his mother's portrait. Her painted amber eyes sparked, no doubt merely a reflection of flickering candlelight.

"I'll be the *greatest* ruler, you'll see. Return in a year's time. And be prepared." He spun on his heel and left with Prince Consentido pouting behind him.

In the course of that year, King Mandamás wasted no time in unleashing his brutality. If someone looked at him the wrong way, he plucked out their eyes. If offended by someone's words, he extracted their teeth, one by one. And then their tongue.

Fear and horror billowed through the kingdom like smoke.

While King Mandamás carried out his increasingly savage acts, Señora Alma continued honing her enigmatic craft.

As it had always been for generations of her family, no one was allowed to enter her studio—her methods were secret. Canvas after canvas of life-size animal portraits encircled the humble space. None were of noble pets or well-bred steeds as one might expect. Instead, they were strikingly realistic representations of common sewer rats and rabid raccoons, all with a spark in their painted eyes. In the center of the room rested a battered cage containing the still-warm carcass of a bloodthirsty coyote, its just-completed portrait looming on an easel nearby. The legendary artist never practiced by painting people, the reason known only to her.

When the year passed, Señora Alma arrived at the palace bringing art materials, a weathered easel, and an enormous blank canvas.

King Mandamás glared from the summit of his throne. "You *shall* paint my portrait this time." At that, guards stepped forward in unison and surrounded her, their swords clanking against their armor.

Señora Alma placed her cane to the side. "As you wish, Your Highness. It is clear to all what kind of ruler you have become, and so I shall *gladly* capture your likeness."

The entire court gathered as Señora Alma stood still and closed her eyes. While she took slow breaths, the watching crowds held theirs. Suddenly, her eyes flashed open, focused on the king. Without breaking her gaze, she thrust out her hand, playing her fingers across her brushes the way a musician tests the keys of a harpsichord. Selecting a bold brush, she began painting the curve of his shoulder.

When the pigment-tipped brush touched the blank canvas, the king twitched and slapped his shoulder. As a slight numbness spread down his arm, he suspected a bee had stung him, but he held his pose—a king isn't bothered by an insignificant bee.

However, as Señora Alma continued, the king faltered. Why, just as the master painter applied the perfect rose tones to the canvas, the king's rosy cheeks paled. And as she dabbed crimson on the lips of his depiction, King Mandamás's own mouth began to blend away into his increasingly sallow complexion.

Murmurs spread. "Look! He *is* cursed for having his portrait painted too soon." The onlookers gasped. "Just like his grandfather!"

Señora Alma smiled to herself. This enduring, false rumor of a curse masked the truth and served her well. She alone knew the power she possessed.

"I'm fine!" the king protested when asked about his health. But something wasn't right. Increasingly drained of his vitality, he knew no bee sting could have this effect. It sent a shiver through his heart. Was it poison? A plague? No matter what, he could display no weakness. He knew any hint of vulnerability would be his end—his enemies would pounce. Now delusional, he even feared his own son, Prince Consentido, might snatch the throne.

But the young prince only gaped in confusion. "Father, is it the curse? You must stop!"

Paranoid and suspecting a trick, King Mandamás flapped his hand at Señora Alma. "Quick, *old woman*, paint swiftly. I want this finished."

She stood tall. "Certainly, Your Highness, I'm sure we all want this *finished*."

The faster she progressed, the more rapidly the king faded. Fortunately, Señora Alma was able to complete his portrait *just* in time. For as she applied two last dabs of paint to the pupils of his eyes, he slumped to the ground. Dead.

Trembling with shock, Prince Consentido approached his father's Funeral Portrait—something about the painting's lifelike gaze pulled at him, almost against his will.

Señora Alma placed a surprisingly firm hand on the boy's shoulder and whispered. "Your Majesty, we will be eagerly observing. What kind of ruler will you be?"

As the boy stared at the painting, a small drop of red paint puddled in the rim of the portrait's right eye, then ran down the flat cheek like a teardrop of blood.

"I wonder when I will paint you," Señora Alma said, searching the boy's face. "When shall I capture *your* soul?"

THE CARVED BEAR
By Brendan Reichs

The little wooden bear had twinkling eyes made of shiny blue glass.

A brown nose. Cute, rounded belly. Small enough to fit in one's palm, it sat on the craftswoman's cart with its front paws extended, as if seeking a hug, its chiseled lips tilted in a shy smile.

Yet something about the carving unsettled Cara. Looking again, she saw that the bear's mouth wasn't grinning so much as leering. Sharp teeth lurked like tiny diamonds. The eyebrows angled downward slightly in what felt like a glare. Its miniature paws were tipped by delicate claws, as likely to rend as to embrace.

A chill traveled down Cara's spine. It was just a silly carving, but she felt like the bear's eyes followed her as she backed away from the rickety old cart parked at the edge of the village market. Cara decided she wanted to be somewhere else.

Her brother, Elam, felt no such discomfort. He was staring at the wooden bear, a greedy glint to his sharp green eyes. Cara began to worry. Elam didn't have any money, but that hadn't always stopped him in the past when he wanted something. And right then, it looked as if Elam really wanted the carved wooden bear.

Cara tugged on her brother's sleeve. "Come on, Elam. Let's go. We're late for home."

Elam nodded, but his eyes never left the cart. A whip cracked behind her and Cara spun, her nerves on edge. It was only a passing coach. When she turned back, Elam was hurrying into the road, his hands shoved deeply into the pockets of his trousers.

Cara experienced a moment of panic. She lurched after him, but guilt caused her to glance back over her shoulder. She froze. The craftswoman was glowering in their direction as Elam scurried away. Cara stiffened—*stupid Elam and his stupid sticky fingers!* But the dark-eyed woman merely shook her head once and turned away, releasing Cara from the prison of her icy gaze as she addressed a potential customer.

Cara sagged in relief, then sped after Elam, her anger growing with every step.

"Elam!" she hissed when she drew alongside him. "What did you do?"

"Nothing." But he wouldn't meet her eye. As twins they could never lie to each other. She always knew when Elam did, and, for her part, Cara always told the truth.

"Elam, that woman *saw* you," Cara breathed. She still couldn't believe the crone hadn't pursued them. Why had she let Elam steal from her? How did he always get so lucky?

"She didn't, or she'd have come after me," Elam said. A nasty smirk stole across his face. "Because I *do* have something she'll miss." He pulled the wooden bear from his pocket and bounced it in one hand.

Cara's temper flared white-hot again, but it quickly blurred to confusion. The bear her brother was casually tossing wasn't the one she'd seen on the cart. The blue eyes were the same, but this bear was frowning darkly, its bushy arms crossed over its chest. Had there been two carvings, and she'd seen only one?

"Come on," Elam said, jamming the pilfered carving back into his pocket. "We *are* late, and I want to play with my new friend later. If you weren't such a priss, you'd have one too."

Elam picked up the pace, forcing Cara to trot along the packed dirt road.

Neither spoke for the rest of the long walk home.

Elam was cheerful throughout dinner, complimenting their mother's cooking and nodding at their father's sage advice. Cara fumed silently, upset by the world's unfairness. Her brother *always* got away with everything. She never broke the rules, but where did that get her? Nowhere, as far she could tell—not an ounce of credit in the twelve years she and Elam had been vying for their parents' attention.

Elam glanced at her once, and stuck his tongue out when their parents weren't looking. He knew his sister would never snitch, no matter what, and was enjoying her foul mood. Cara sank deeper into her chair and gnawed grimly on a carrot.

After dinner, the twins finished their chores and were given free time to play. Elam produced his stolen bear and pranced it around the parlor, making it say funny things and caper wildly before the fire. Their parents laughed, accepting his story of a lucky find down by the river. Cara bit her tongue and tried to read, but the fairy tales had lost their appeal.

Finally, it was bedtime. "No playthings during rest hours," their father admonished sternly. Elam set the wooden bear on the mantel and scampered to the twins' shared bedroom. After washing, they both climbed into their beds, one smilingly smug, the other thoroughly annoyed and grateful for the day's end. The lamps were doused, and Cara hunted for the release of sleep.

She'd nearly drifted off when a floorboard creaked outside their bedroom door.

She sat up in bed, and felt Elam do the same. "Pa?" he called out.

No answer came. Cara felt a chill lift the hairs on her neck, the same ill feeling she'd had by the craftswoman's cart. She heard Elam grumble, get out of bed, and light a candle. The slender flame bobbed toward the door. Elam opened it, then sucked in a breath of surprise.

The little wooden bear was in the center of the hallway just outside their door. The figurine gleamed, as if drawing in the candlelight. But even stranger, Cara noticed that it was now down on all fours, its face locked in a snarl. The blue eyes glittered.

Elam lifted the carving, scratching his head. "Weird. Does this look different to you?" he asked his sister.

Cara was nearly unable to answer. "I think you should take it back," she whispered.

"Take it back?" Elam shot her a disgusted look. "After all the trouble I went through to steal it? Who would do such a thing?" He squinted down at the bear, then shook his head. "I wonder why Ma put it out here?"

Before Cara could answer, Elam slapped it on the dresser beside the door. Then he trudged back to bed, got under the covers, and blew out the candle. In moments, light snores rose from his pile of blankets.

Cara found sleep more elusive. She couldn't stop thinking about the bear, or the craftswoman's dire expression as she turned away. Had the bear really changed shape since Elam took it without paying? She wished he hadn't brought it into their bedroom.

Her weariness finally won over and she fell into a dreamless slumber. But a short time later another floorboard groaned, this time *inside* their room.

Cara shot up in bed, an unknown dread squeezing her heart. Her ears detected a scurrying sound and she broke into a cold sweat. "Elam! Wake up!" she whisper-shouted.

Elam rolled over on his pillow. "What is it? Why are you bothering me now?"

"Light the candle, Elam."

"What?"

"Just do it!"

After a string of petulant curses, Cara heard Elam fumbling with the matches. Candlelight bloomed, forming a pale circle. Cara leaned over and peered into the gloom.

The little wooden bear was in the center of the floor between their beds. The carving now stood on its hind legs, paws raised and gleaming claws extended, its jaws cracked in what could only be a fearsome growl.

Cara felt her blood run cold. "Elam, the bear. It *moved*. And changed shape again!"

"Don't be silly," Elam scoffed, but his voice carried a quiver. "It's a carving. Candlelight fools the eye, is all."

Cara shook her head. "Elam, it was on the dresser! You need to get rid of it. Put it outside somewhere, and then take it back tomorrow."

Elam's head whipped around, eyes narrowing. "I see your plan, sister," he snarled. "You think to prank me with my own prize, so that I take it back like a dimwit. You're jealous, so you're playing a cruel game in the dark while I sleep."

Cara's eyes widened. "Elam, no! I swear it!"

Elam hopped out of bed and kicked the wooden bear into the corner of the room. "Enough. The bear is mine. I stole it clean. Now leave off and go to bed. If you don't, you'll find your dolls floating in the well tomorrow."

"Elam, please! I didn't tou—"

"Not one more word!" He blew out the candle and

yanked a blanket over his head.

Cara choked back a panicked moan. She'd only wake their parents, and they'd be angry with her for disturbing their rest. Plus, they'd never believe her story. Cara wasn't sure of it herself. Maybe a draft had blown the bear off the dresser? Maybe its face got chipped in the fall, making her see things that weren't there?

With no other recourse, Cara pulled her covers tight and hid her face, praying for morning to come. She vowed not to sleep at all, perking her ears and listening for the slightest sound. She heard nothing for hours. Then her body betrayed her and Cara dozed off.

She awoke to the first slanting rays of dawn. Yawning, it took her a moment to remember her fright from the night before. She scrambled upright and looked to her brother, but the pile of blankets still covered his bed completely.

Cara began to feel very foolish. She glanced at the corner where the wooden bear had been kicked. Then she squinted in confusion.

It wasn't there.

Cara turned back to her brother's bed. The chill returned, deeper than ever before, seeping all the way down to her bones. Cara took a calming breath, reached over, and pulled back the covers.

Dark stains covered the sheets, which were torn to shreds. A pillow had been ripped open, its feathers sticking in viscous liquid. In the center of it all was the little wooden bear, its body dyed scarlet from the waist down. Angry red smears covered its mouth and claws. The carving reclined on its back with its tongue lolling out, both hands wrapped around its belly. A wicked smile split its face, but it didn't touch those cold blue eyes.

Cara screamed.

Her parents rushed in and shouted in horror, demanding to know where Elam was, but Cara snatched the bear and ran from the room without speaking a word. She bolted out of the house, down the road, and all the long way back to where the craftswoman's cart had been the day before.

But when she arrived, the cart was gone, only muddy ruts signifying it had ever existed. Cara sat down and began to cry, flinging the bear to the ground in helpless despair. She heard it thud against something else. Dabbing her eyes, she spotted another wooden carving lying in the wet grass. She lifted it clear and wiped it with her fingers.

It was a blond-haired boy with polished green eyes, standing in denim overalls.

"*Elam*," Cara breathed, her pulse thundering.

The boy's engraved face stretched in an expression of horror, its hands reaching out as if for help. Cara hugged the carving to her chest and sobbed silently. Then she put the tiny figurine in her pocket and started the long walk home.

She didn't tell her distraught parents what happened. They'd never believe her. Instead, she set the statue of her brother on the dresser, where the bear had been, and crawled into bed, shuddering at the blank space where Elam's mattress should have been. Sleep took her immediately, and it was several hours before she blinked awake.

Cara sat up. Felt a prickle run down her back.

She looked over and found the statue of her brother sitting on her bedside table.

The boy was now leaning back with his ankles crossed, smirking, one wooden finger resting on its opposite shoulder. As Cara watched, unable to blink, the finger slid slowly across the statue's neck. A green eye winked, then froze in place.

Cara swallowed. Fresh tears spilled from her eyes.

She lifted the carving to her lips and kissed it once.

Then she walked to the living room and tossed it into the roaring fireplace.

DON'T YOU SEE THAT CAT?
By Gaby Triana

The tall figure floated in like a ghost, breaking her concentration. "This is the last time I'm going to tell you." It was her mother, speaking calmly—too calmly. "Please take out the trash."

Kendra sighed and placed her pencil in her math book. "Yes, Mom."

She went into the kitchen, closed up a full garbage bag, and dragged it out the front door. Dumping the trash into a side bin, she paused when she noticed something.

By the wheat field across the street was a skinny cat she'd never seen before. Its fur was orange and looked like it'd gotten into a skirmish with a pair of rusted scissors. The scruffy thing stared at Kendra without moving a muscle. Around it, tall wheat swayed in the late-afternoon breeze. Crows skittered beside it, pecking at grain.

Kendra's mother appeared in the doorway. "What is it?"

"That cat." Kendra pointed. "Don't you see it?"

When Kendra blinked, however, the cat was gone.

"No." Her mother shrugged. "Come back inside. It's getting chilly."

The next day, Kendra was walking home from school when she saw it again. Like the day before, the old cat sat by the wheat field, watching her carefully without moving a muscle. All around it, crows pecked at grain, unbothered.

Kendra squatted. "Here, kitty," she called. The animal sat tall and still. It looked even more beat-up and skinnier than before. Kendra went into the house and stole some ham from the refrigerator.

"Where are you going with that?" her mother asked.

"To feed the cat."

"I'd rather you not." Her mother followed her to the front porch. "Where is it?"

"Right there. Don't you see it?" Kendra pointed across the street.

"No, I don't."

Kendra was puzzled. "It's right there." She placed the ham on the front steps and waited, but the cat would not cross the street. After a minute, Kendra pouted and went back inside. When she glanced through the window minutes later, the cat was gone. At night, the ham was still there, uneaten, covered in ants.

The next day, Kendra did her math homework while wondering about the strange cat. An autumn breeze billowed the kitchen curtains. Chilled, she stood and leaned to the window to close it.

There it was again—the shabby cat. This time, it sat in the middle of the road.

"It's back!" Kendra ran to the front door, her heart pounding.

Her mother followed. "All right, let's see this thing once and for all."

But by the time they both stepped onto the porch, the cat had disappeared again.

"It was just here! Sitting in the street. I promise!" Kendra frowned. She knew she had seen the same cat with the tattered, dusty coat. It glared at her the way Mrs. Nottage glared whenever Kendra wouldn't stop talking in class.

"Well, it better be careful," her mom warned. "A few days ago, a stray was hit by a car just down the street. An accident, of course. This is a dangerous road."

Kendra wanted to break down crying. Every time she saw the cat, it disappeared before her mother could see it. Was it even real? Of course it was. She'd seen it three times already. So why did she feel like her mother didn't believe her?

That evening, Kendra was getting ready for bed when a cold gust of wind rattled her bedroom shutters. She was about to close them when she froze. That mangy old cat was sitting on her wooden fence. As always, it stared at her—*through* her. Now that it had come closer, Kendra could see the cat's coat wasn't just old, it was matted with dirt, and one of its eyes looked glued shut. The other appeared yellow.

Kendra shivered. This time, she did not call her mother.

She locked the window and nervously slipped into bed.

On her nightstand, the clock ticked and ticked. A tree outside created long shadows on her bedroom wall. Creaky branches scraped against the house. Kendra ran to the window, tugged the curtains together, then jumped back into bed, pulling the covers over her head. After a while, she fell asleep.

Then, she heard it—a low yowl. *Mrrooowwwww...*

Her eyes popped open. Kendra flew to the window and parted the curtains with shaky hands. There was that dreaded cat again, sitting on the slope of the roof a few feet from her window. Was it following her? Why did it keep staring at her like that?

Closer now, its fur not only appeared dark, matted, and dusty, but . . .

Kendra swallowed.

Squeezing her eyes shut, she tried to erase what she'd seen. Half the cat's fur was covered in dried blood. She climbed back into bed, pulling the covers up to her chin. She never should have put that ham out. She never should have called to the stray cat. Now it would not leave her alone.

After a long while, all noises stopped except for the clock's ticking. Kendra fell back asleep and dreamed about the strange animal from the wheat field. The one even the crows did not seem to see. The cat in the road. The cat on her fence. The cat on her roof.

What did it want?

Finally, in the middle of the night, she awoke to a horrible sound in the stillness of her room—the low yowl again. *Mrrooowwwww* . . . Kendra's skin felt like the uneaten ham slice crawling with ants. Then, something jumped onto her bed, something small and light on its four feet.

Paws pressed along her legs, then came to sit in the middle of her chest. Shaking, Kendra slowly pulled the covers off her eyes, knowing in her heart what it was—the cat, the ratty wounded cat that had been stalking her for days.

But nothing was there.

She sat up, switched on the light, expecting to see the curtains and window open. They were still shut. So she'd been dreaming? Kendra breathed a sigh of relief.

Then, along the rug, she couldn't believe what she spotted. Paw prints. Dark. Red. Dirty. And on her blanket—a dead, bloody crow.

THE GOLDEN PEACOCK
By Alethea Kontis

Gus and Angela Vasilakis inherited the painting from one of Angela's great-aunts. The frame itself was nondescript: a plain square of rough wood, about an arm's length on each side. But inside that frame, painstakingly crafted from pigmented oils, was the gorgeously rendered eye of one feather from a golden peacock.

Ancient Greeks said that the eyes that decorate a peacock's feathers were a tribute to the hundred-eyed giant who had faithfully served as the goddess Hera's watchdog. The feather's eye in this painting, however, was based on the eye of a real-life girl, an Ottoman Greek descendant of the Byzantine emperors.

Some of Angela's relatives said that the girl had perished in the fires of the Greek genocide. Others argued that the painting was older, saying that the girl had lived during the reign of the Trebizond Empire. No one had so much as a clue about the painter, but all the stories agreed on one thing: that the girl's name was Melora.

Melora's eye had watched over Angela's family for as long as anyone could remember. Not that it mattered—to the casual observer, the painting looked like nothing more than a close-up of a beautiful shimmering peacock feather.

The painting had hung prominently over the old aunt's fireplace until she passed away.

Gus and Angela had a baby—a happy little girl named Phoebe, with a head full of white-golden ringlets and eyes the color of polished olivewood. When Angela received the painting, she and her husband hung it in Phoebe's room, so that Melora could watch over their precious daughter. The bright peacock's feather looked right at home above Phoebe's dresser.

When Phoebe was four, she began telling stories about an imaginary friend named Melora.

"Sweetheart, where did you hear the name Melora?" asked Angela.

"Melora told me," Phoebe answered.

Gus decided to play along. "Where did you meet Melora?"

"Here. In my room," said Phoebe. "She's always been here." The way she said it made it sound like a fact, and not like she was playing pretend.

It creeped Gus out. "Did you tell her about the painting in her room?" he asked his wife.

"I don't remember." Angela shrugged. "Maybe?"

"Your family has a million stories about this painting. Do any of them sound like this?" Gus asked, nodding at their daughter.

"No," said Angela.

When Phoebe was five, she grew a stubborn streak. In turn, according to Phoebe, Melora had become just as argumentative as her playmate.

One particularly quiet day, Gus went into Phoebe's bedroom in search of his daughter and found Phoebe playing in the closet.

"Why are you in here, pumpkin?"

"Melora got mad and said I had to stay in here," said Phoebe.

"Aren't imaginary friends supposed to be nice?" Gus asked his daughter.

"Melora's not imaginary," said Phoebe. "She just *is.*"

Gus wasn't sure what to say to that. He did not understand imaginary playmates, but he understood bullies. "Well, the next time you two fight, tell her that it's *her* turn to stay in the closet."

"Okay, Daddy."

Later that night, well past her bedtime, Phoebe

turned up in her parents' room.

"What's the matter, sweetheart?" asked Angela.

"I can't sleep," said Phoebe. "Melora's crying."

"Why is Melora crying?" asked Angela.

"Daddy told me to lock her in the closet next time we fought. She's been crying for *hours*. She says I'm not fair."

Gus sighed at his daughter's imagination. "That's not Melora, honey, that's just the rain. It's storming outside. Just ignore it. I promise it will be over soon."

"Yes, Daddy," Phoebe said.

The next night, Phoebe was back. "I can't sleep," she told her parents. "Melora keeps calling my name and won't stop. She says she's going to keep me awake all night long."

"It's the wind," said Angela. "Just ignore it."

"It will stop as soon as you go to sleep, pumpkin," said Gus. "I promise."

"Yes, Daddy," Phoebe said.

The third night, Phoebe was back again. "Melora's scratching at the door. She says she's going to scratch me."

"I'll be glad when she grows out of this Melora business," said Angela.

"It's just her imagination," said Gus. "I'll handle it."

He got out of bed and went into Phoebe's bedroom to investigate. The streetlamp shone through the tree outside the window, casting a pattern of shadows across the walls. The room was a little cold, but not uncomfortably so.

Gus tried to see the room through the eyes of a scared five-year-old. The closet door was open a crack—he shut it. He went through the motions of checking under the bed for monsters. Then he heard it . . . a soft *scratch, scratch, scratch.*

Phoebe and her father both jumped at the sound.

"Melora's coming to get me," Phoebe whispered.

When Gus's heart stopped pounding, he noticed the shadows in the room shifting. Laughing, he pulled back the sheer curtain. "It's just the tree outside, pumpkin," said Gus.

Phoebe tried to laugh too.

"See? The branches here keep brushing up against the window. That's what's making the sound. Just pretend you are rock-a-bye baby, being rocked to sleep in the treetop."

"Okay, Daddy," said Phoebe.

Gus and Angela put heavier curtains in Phoebe's room to block out the shadows and sounds from the street. Angela also gave Phoebe one of her silky spa masks to sleep in. She told her daughter it was magic.

It must have worked, because Phoebe did not appear in their room that night. Or the next night.

On the third night, Gus stuck his head into his daughter's room to check on her. Phoebe was not in her bed. After a terrified minute of frantic searching, Gus found Phoebe *under* the bed.

"Hey, pumpkin, it's Daddy," Gus said. "What are you doing under the bed?"

Phoebe slid the overly large sleeping mask up to peek at her father. "Melora doesn't like my mask," she said. "It makes her say mean things."

Gus was really starting to worry about his daughter's big imagination. "What kind of mean things, pumpkin? Did she say she was going to scratch you again?"

"She says she's going to tear out my eyes," said Phoebe. "I'm hiding down here so she can't find me."

Gus glanced around the dark, empty room. "Where is Melora right now, pumpkin?"

"She looks at me through the painting." Phoebe's tiny arm pointed to the peacock feather on the wall above her dresser. "She's always watching."

"That's it," said Gus. "I've had enough." And with that, he took the painting down off the wall.

"What are you going to do with that?" Angela asked when she saw him with the painting.

"I'm going to put it in the garage," he said. "I don't even want it in this house anymore."

Angela smirked. "Just don't tell my aunts and uncles. They love that stupid painting. They practically worship the thing."

"Then they can have it!" Gus yelled as he walked out the door.

The next morning, Phoebe came out of her room with the magical sleeping mask still over her eyes.

"Did you get a good night's sleep, pumpkin?" Gus asked.

"Yes, Daddy," Phoebe said, "but I need Mommy to help me with the magic mask. I can't take it off."

Gus reached down and removed his daughter's mask.

Angela screamed.

"Can you take the mask off, Mommy?" Phoebe asked again.

But the mask was off.

Phoebe's beautiful olive eyes were gone.

There was nothing beneath her flaccid eyelids but two gaping sockets of bloody, raw flesh.

Gus ran out of the house. As much as he hated that horrible painting, and whatever wretched ghost of a girl lived inside it, he would hang it over the fireplace in a solid gold frame if it meant his daughter could have her eyes back. He searched the garage from top to bottom.

The painting was nowhere to be found.

So next time you visit a museum, or stay at a hotel, look to see if the painting is there. Every garage sale you go to, be sure to keep an eye out. The frame might have changed, but the painting will be the same: a young girl's eye, staring, unblinking, from the feather of a golden peacock. And if you ever happen to find it, be sure that it is hung in a place of importance and treated with the greatest respect.

Because the next pair of eyes Melora takes *could be yours*!

THE KNOCK-KNOCK MAN
by Brenna Yovanoff

The mirror sat in the back corner of the attic, leaning against the wall next to where the chimney stuck out. It was big, much bigger than the one in the bathroom downstairs. Almost as big as a doorway.

Hailey sat in front of it, balanced on an old milk crate full of dusty jigsaw puzzles. The attic was the size of Arizona, with low slanted ceilings and a little round window at one end, like a porthole. It was strange that she'd never noticed the mirror before. She played up here a lot, digging through stacks of her mother's old magazines.

Their neighborhood was nice, full of cottonwood trees and rambling parks, but mostly she stayed in the house. Her mother didn't like for her to leave the yard alone.

The reason, her mother said, was that there were snakes down in the ditch sometimes, and the big road out by the edge of the development was too busy.

But Hailey knew that the real reason was Cathy.

All her life, Hailey had heard stories about the terrible thing that had happened. The awful tragedy of her mother's kidnapped sister. It was creepy but familiar, like the safety assemblies they had sometimes at school—all the warnings and the rules. Never tell anyone your name or let the neighbors know you're home alone. Never talk to strangers. There were bad people in the world, waiting to snatch up little girls. It was just much safer to stay in the house.

In the mirror, Hailey's reflection was softer than usual, like seeing herself through a piece of lace. There was a layer of dust on the glass, turning the room behind her warm and blurry. It made her eyes look greener than they were.

The way the mirror leaned lazily against the wall made her feel expected, like it had been waiting here all this time. Like a special present, just for her.

"There's a mirror in the attic," she said to her mother.

They were in the kitchen, under the cut-glass ceiling lamp. On other nights, when the sky was low and it got dark early, Hailey would be hunched over the table finishing her homework. But now it was summer and there were no long division sets to do, no questions about Gettysburg, so she sat in the yellow glow of the light, peeling glitter polish off her fingernails.

Her mother looked up from a stack of receipts. "What mirror?"

Hailey shrugged. "A fancy one. With a big carved flower on top."

Hailey's mother pursed her lips. "Oh." Then she leafed through the receipts again, like she was counting them. "That was your aunt Cathy's," she said without looking at Hailey. "She used to have it in her bedroom."

She said it in a flat, final way that Hailey was used to. Her mother always sounded half asleep when she talked about Cathy. Hailey waited, but this time her mother didn't say the other things. That the world outside was too noisy and too big, too full of monsters. You could never be sure who the bad men were. That the juniper bushes that looked so green and lovely from the window might hide a man with knives, a man who watched with hot, angry eyes, then came to your door in the night and took you.

When Hailey was little, her mother had called him the Knock-Knock Man.

Back then, the bad things all seemed far away and the fenced-in yard had still appeared big enough to hold her. She'd made up games and played them by herself, racing through the grass with a sheet tied around her neck like a cape. The games were always about running away. Pirates who stole girls from their beds and took them on adventures, or wicked fairies, or Robin Hood. In her games, she was an explorer, brave and intrepid. She would never be lonely or afraid. The Knock-Knock Man was only a dark, smudgy shape somewhere in the distance.

Hailey peeled the last strip of glitter polish off her pinkie nail and didn't look up.

That night she stared at the wall, thinking about the mirror. It looked much too big for someone to have carried it up the narrow stairs to the attic. She wondered how it had gotten there. She pictured it hanging in a bedroom, in some other house, while the girl who lived there—Cathy, maybe—danced and slept and brushed her hair and sang along to all her favorite songs.

Hailey was twelve now, but in another month, she'd be thirteen. She'd be older than Cathy had been on the day she disappeared. Hailey never danced or played pirates anymore. When she fell asleep, she dreamed about a place where the curtains were always closed and none of the rooms had doors. The air was dry and muffling. You couldn't hear the road. A house so clean and quiet, it could have been made of paper.

The mirror was hard to stay away from.

That was the strangest part.

The scary part was that she didn't try.

The next morning, as soon as she'd eaten breakfast and put her bowl in the sink, Hailey climbed up to the attic and looked at herself. For a second, the picture in the mirror didn't seem like a reflection at all, but like she was seeing someone through a window.

There was a dark smudge in the corner of the glass, shaped like a tall, bony shadow, but when Hailey turned to look behind her, there was nothing there.

The smudge made her think of a skeletal figure. A shambling man, coming up behind her. She couldn't see the thing's face, but she could almost feel it seeing hers.

When she turned back to the mirror, the mark was gone. There was only her reflection.

The girl in the mirror had a soft, round face—too cute to really be pretty. Hailey pressed her hands against her cheeks to make them flatter. So did the girl in the mirror. When Hailey stopped, her reflection stopped too. Together, they sat staring at each other, toying with the messy sheaf of hair that hung over their shoulders.

It was a second before Hailey could work out why that was strange.

Then she froze. The girl in the mirror had the same bony wrists, the same square hands, little flecks of glitter still stuck to the fingernails. But Hailey's own hair was pulled back in a ponytail.

That was impossible. She closed her eyes, and when she opened them again, her reflection was looking back at her, calm as glass, everything in its place—freckles, cheeks. Ponytail. Everything where it should be.

"Knock, knock," she whispered. She could feel the way her mouth moved—the shape of the words as she said them—but in the mirror, it looked like the girl was saying something else.

⁂

It wasn't real, the thing she'd seen in the mirror. She knew that.

Reflections weren't like videos or photographs—you couldn't fake them with angles or computers. They might warp or bend things like the fun-house mirrors at the fair, but they didn't show you with your hair down when it wasn't. They could be stretched or blurry, but they still basically showed you what was true. Anything else was a trick of the light. The dark, shambling smudge in the corner had just been a trick of the light.

But still, the mirror made her nervous. She spent

the afternoon downstairs.

When Wendy Tally's mom called to see if Hailey wanted to come with them to the swimming pool, she took a long time to answer the phone. The house felt backward and confusing, like everything was flipped around. Doors that looked right at first all led away from the places she wanted to go. She wasn't sure how the rooms connected.

Trying to figure it out made her head ache. She said goodbye to Mrs. Tally, then followed the tangled pattern in the hallway carpet until she found the living room, where she sat on the couch and waited for her ears to stop buzzing. She'd seen pictures of her aunt Cathy at her grandmother's house, in the big old album with the fake leather cover. Now she sat, trying to remember what they had looked like. The thing she was almost sure of was that the girl in the pictures had looked a lot like Hailey.

She decided she would rather stay inside.

Hailey was in the attic again. She didn't know how long she'd been there. Her legs felt tingly and numb. The light had changed. Everything was darker.

The girl in the mirror wasn't her anymore. At least, not the way a reflection was supposed to be. Instead, there were a pair of girls who looked alike, with the same scattered freckles and soft, tangly hair. The same small, straight noses. Hailey, and a girl she'd only ever known from her grandmother's faded photographs. Just a girl who'd gone missing one hot July day a long time ago. They didn't look like reflections at all, they looked like sisters.

"What are you doing in there?" Hailey asked. Her voice sounded flat and far away.

"Hiding from the Knock-Knock Man," Cathy said. "The only way to hide from him is to stay inside."

The room in the mirror looked nicer than the one that she was in.

Cathy leaned closer, reaching out. "It's safe in here. It's perfect. If you give me your hand, you can come too."

Hailey reached back. Under her palms, the glass felt colder than it should have. It was chilly where Cathy was. It didn't make sense, but Hailey couldn't remember why. "Aren't you lonely in there? Aren't you stuck?"

Cathy smiled and shook her head. "I'm safe."

"You were kidnapped, though. You were missing. I don't understand."

"You will."

The room in the mirror was bright and much too clean. Hailey leaned closer. She had never wanted to be safe inside a glass house before. She had never wanted so much quiet.

They leaned toward each other. Cathy's face seemed to ripple. Hailey saw a kind of wild joy there, savage and hungry, and then she understood.

There was no Knock-Knock Man. At least, not the way her mother was afraid of, not hiding in the dark to steal girls. There was only this—a silent, stifling place where nothing got lost or old or dirty and nothing changed.

Hailey felt the glass go slippery and soft, like it was melting into water. She closed her eyes. When a hard, cold hand closed around her wrist, she felt lonely and small and very afraid, but she did not feel surprised.

"Knock, knock," Cathy whispered.

STRANGE MUSIC
By Joanna Parypinski